TAKE TED INSTEAD

For Jazzy, Ryder and Aurora. CW

For Patrick. AF

First published in the UK in 2017
by New Frontier Publishing Pty Ltd
93 Harbord Street, London SW6 6PN
www.newfrontierpublishing.co.uk

ISBN: 978-1-912076-61-1

A CIP catalogue record for this book is available from the British Library.

Designed by Celeste Hulme

Printed in China
10 9 8 7 6 5 4 3 2 1

TAKE TED INSTEAD

Cassandra Webb ★ Illustrated by Amanda Francey

NEW FRONTIER PUBLISHING

It's time for bed, sleepy head.

No, no, take **RED** instead.

It's time for bed, sleepy head.

No, no, take **SEB** instead.

It's time for bed, sleepy head.

No, no, take **FRED** instead.

It's time for bed, sleepy head.

No, no, take **JEDD** instead.

It's time for bed, sleepy head.

No, no, take **ZED** instead.

It's time for bed, sleepy head.

No, no, take
NED
instead.

It's time for bed, sleepy head.

No, no, take **ED** instead.

It's time for bed,
sleepy head.

No, no, take **TED** instead.

But Ted will be lonely,
in bed all on his own.

Take **ME** too.